P9-DXT-668

# Disney

# MICKEY AND MINNIE

## READ-AND-LISTEN
### STORYBOOK

Disney PRESS

New York • Los Angeles

"A Perfect Picnic" written by Kate Ritchey. Illustrated by Loter, Inc.,
and the Disney Storybook Art Team.

"A Summer Day" adapted from the story "Donald Takes a Trip" by Kate Ritchey.
Illustrated by Loter, Inc., and the Disney Storybook Art Team.

"The Birthday Surprise" written by Elle D. Risco. Illustrated by Loter, Inc.,
and the Disney Storybook Art Team.

For information address Disney Press, 1101 Flower Street, Glendale, California 91201.
Printed in China
First Edition
1 3 5 7 9 10 8 6 4 2
F383-2370-2-14080
ISBN 978-1-4847-0436-3

# CONTENTS

# DISNEY

# MICKEY MOUSE

# THE PET SHOW

It was a perfect day for a cookout. Mickey Mouse and his nephews, Morty and Ferdie, were preparing lunch when Minnie arrived.

"I'm sorry I'm late," she said, "but I have great news. I've just been elected chairperson of the Charity Pet Show. We're raising money to build a new shelter for stray animals."

"We should enter Pluto in the show!" Morty suggested.

"Yeah! We can teach him to do tricks," said Ferdie. "Watch this!"

Mickey and Minnie watched as the boys tried to train Pluto for the show.

"Roll over, Pluto," Morty said.

But Pluto just sat up and wagged his tail.

"Maybe we should *show* him what we want him to do," said Ferdie.

Pluto watched, puzzled, as both boys rolled over in the grass.

"Hmmm. That didn't work, either," Ferdie said.

Then Morty had an idea. "Let's try something that *Pluto* likes to do," he suggested.

Ferdie ordered Pluto to lie down, but Pluto
jumped up and began chasing his tail instead.

All week long, Morty and Ferdie tried to teach
Pluto new tricks.

He fetched.

He rolled over.

And he shook hands . . . . but
only when he wanted to.

On the day of the show, Minnie sold Mickey three tickets. While the boys rushed off to get Pluto ready, Minnie pointed happily to the cashbox.

"We've made enough to pay for the new animal shelter!" she told Mickey.

"That's great!" cried Mickey.

What *wasn't* great was Pluto's performance.

He shook hands when he was told to sit. He
rolled over when he should have jumped. And he
barked when he was supposed to lie down. Worst
of all, when Police Chief O'Hara was choosing the
Best Pet of the Day, Pluto *growled* at him! The chief
didn't know it, but he was standing right where Pluto
had buried his bone!

Suddenly the crowd heard a scream from the ticket booth.

"Help! Stop, thief! Help!"

"That's Minnie!" Mickey gasped.

"The ticket money!" Morty and Ferdie shouted.

Mickey, the boys, and Chief O'Hara ran to the booth.

Pluto was already at the scene of the crime. He
was busily sniffing around.

"All the money is gone," Minnie said. "I walked
away for one minute. When I came back, I saw
someone running away with the cashbox."

"What did the robber look like?" asked the chief. Before Minnie could answer, Pluto took off.

"He's tracking the thief!" shouted Mickey.

A moment later, the thief ran screaming out of the woods. He was holding on to the cashbox—and Pluto was holding on to *him*! Pluto growled and tugged on the thief's suspenders.

*S-s-snap!* The thief's suspenders broke and shot him right into the arms of Chief O'Hara.

Later that afternoon, Chief O'Hara presented Pluto with the Four-Footed Hero medal.

The chief smiled and said, "Thanks to Pluto, every animal will have a place to go—and a chance to find a good home."

At home, Pluto waited by the front door.

"You know," said Morty, "I don't care if Pluto isn't a show dog. He's something better. He's a *hero* dog."

Mickey, Minnie, and Ferdie agreed. Then, without being told, Pluto shook hands with everyone, because this time *he* wanted to.

# DISNEY

## MICKEY MOUSE

# A PERFECT PICNIC

It was a beautiful spring day. The sun was shining. The birds were singing. And Mickey Mouse was planning a picnic.

Suddenly, Mickey had an idea.

"Picnics are so much better with company,"
he told Pluto. "Maybe I should invite our friends
to join us. What do you think, boy?"

Pluto barked. He agreed with Mickey.

Mickey picked up the phone and called Goofy.
"Hiya, Goofy," he said. "How would you like to have
a picnic in the park? We can all make our favorite
foods, and then we can swap baskets!"

"Gosh, Mickey," said Goofy. "That sounds fun!
What should I bring?"

Goofy began to list his favorite sandwiches. "Cream cheese and marshmallow? Pickle and honey? Spaghetti and olive?" Suddenly Goofy shouted, "I've got it! I know just what to make. See you at the park, Mickey!" And with that he hung up.

Mickey laughed as he put down the phone. Goofy sure did like some weird foods.

While Goofy made his lunch, Mickey went to invite his other friends to the picnic. First he went to see Minnie.

"Oh, Mickey," Minnie said. "A picnic sounds like a perfect way to spend the day. And sharing all of our favorite foods sounds like so much fun. I can't wait!"

Mickey was on his way to Donald's house
when he ran into Donald and Daisy taking a walk.

"A picnic sounds like a wonderful idea," said
Daisy.

"I know just what to bring!" said Donald.

Donald raced home and began to pack a lunch. He took out two pieces of bread to make a sandwich. He got out his favorite drink. And he chose a piece of fruit.

But as Donald looked at the food, he began to get hungry. These are *my* favorite foods, he thought. I don't want to share them. I want to eat them myself!

Over at Minnie's house, things were not going so well either. Minnie had packed all of her favorite foods: a peanut butter sandwich, lemonade, and an apple. But as she got ready to leave, she started to wonder if she would like the lunches her friends had packed.

I don't want to share my lunch, she thought. I want to eat it myself!

Daisy was excited about sharing her lunch.
She hummed to herself as she packed her sandwich
and drink. Then Daisy picked up a banana. Daisy
thought about someone else eating her favorite fruit
and began to frown. Maybe she didn't want to share
her lunch after all. . . .

Over at Goofy's house, the kitchen
was very messy! Goofy was making lemonade to
take to the picnic. He was soaking wet and covered
in lemon juice!

Goofy tasted his lemonade. It was delicious!

This is my best lemonade ever, Goofy thought.

I don't want to share it. I want to drink it all myself!

Mickey had finished packing his basket and was about to leave his house when Pluto began barking at him. Pluto grabbed Mickey's shorts and tugged.

Mickey followed Pluto into the kitchen.
"Thanks for reminding me," he said, taking out
a bone. "I wouldn't want to forget your lunch!"

Mickey didn't know that his friends had changed their minds. As he walked to the park, he grew more excited about his picnic.

Soon he was skipping and humming to himself.

"Won't this be fun, Pluto?" he said. "I wonder what everyone packed for lunch."

When Mickey got to the park, he found his
friends waiting for him. They all had baskets of food.
But they didn't look very happy.

"What's wrong?" Mickey asked his friends.

"I don't want to share my lunch," Donald said.

"What if I don't like the lunch I get?" asked Minnie.

Daisy and Goofy agreed. Everyone wanted to eat
their own favorite foods.

"Oh," Mickey said, disappointed. "I guess
we don't *have* to share."

Minnie looked at Mickey. He looked so sad. She didn't want to be the reason he was upset!

Minnie handed Mickey her picnic basket. "It's okay, Mickey," she said. "I'll trade lunches with you."

"Really? Thanks, Minnie!" Mickey said.

Mickey's friends saw how happy Minnie had
made Mickey. They wanted to make Mickey happy,
too.

"Will someone trade lunches with me?" Donald
asked, holding out his basket.

Daisy took Donald's lunch. Then she handed her
basket to Goofy and he gave his basket to Donald.

Mickey laid out a blanket and the friends
got to work setting up their picnic.

Minnie passed out plates.

Goofy handed out napkins.

Daisy gave everyone a cup.

And Donald set out forks.

Mickey opened his picnic basket first. When he saw what was inside, he started to laugh.

"What's so funny, Mickey?" Minnie asked. Then she looked in her basket and started to laugh, too.

Everyone had packed peanut butter sandwiches and lemonade!

The only difference in the baskets was the fruit.

Daisy had grapes.

Minnie had an orange.

Goofy had a banana.

Mickey had an apple.

And Donald had a pineapple!

"Isn't there some way we can share our fruit?"
asked Minnie.

"I have an idea," said Mickey. "Leave it to me."

While his friends ate their sandwiches and drank their lemonade, Mickey cut up the fruit. He put it all in a bowl and mixed it together. Then he took the bowl back over to the blanket. He had made a big fruit salad!

"What a great idea," Minnie said as Mickey passed out the fruit salad.

"Now we can all try each other's favorite fruits!" Daisy added.

Donald nodded. "Thanks for inviting us, Mickey," he said.

As Mickey's friends ate their
dessert, they realized that Mickey had
been right. Sharing *was* fun, after all!

# DISNEP

## MINNIE MOUSE

# A GOOD DAY FOR A SAIL

One lovely summer day, Mickey Mouse asked his girlfriend, Minnie, if she'd like to go for a boat ride.

"I would love to," Minnie said with a smile. "A nice, easy ride sounds like the perfect way to spend the day."

Mickey and Minnie were preparing to set sail when Goofy came running by.

"Hiya, Mickey. Hiya, Minnie," he said and waved. "What a great day for a boat ride!"

Goofy was looking at Mickey's boat and didn't see a squirrel crossing his path. He accidentally stepped on its tail.

The squirrel leaped away and landed in the boat.
Minnie and Minnie were so startled that they
jumped up, making the boat rock.

Mickey tried to stop the rocking, but he could not. The boat tipped over, sending Mickey and Minnie into the water.

Donald Duck was nearby in his speedboat and saw what had happened. He helped Mickey and Minnie into his boat. "Why don't you ride with me for a while?" he said. "You can take it easy and let the engine do the work."

Mickey and Minnie sat back and relaxed.
They had just reached the middle of the lake when
the boat's engine suddenly stopped.

"What do we do now?" Minnie asked.

"I have an idea," Donald said. He took off his hat
and started to paddle with it.

Mickey and Minnie did the same. Huffing and
puffing, they made their way back to shore.

"How about some lunch while we dry off?"
Mickey said.

Minnie agreed, and the two were soon relaxing
in the sun with hot dogs.

As they were enjoying their lunch, Pluto came
running by. When he saw the delicious hot dogs, he
decided he wanted one, too. He jumped into Mickey's
lap and tried to grab the food.

"Stop it, boy!" cried Mickey.

"Pluto," said Minnie, "if you want a hot dog, we can get you one."

But it was too late. Pluto knocked Mickey and Minnie right into the water!

Mickey and Minnie climbed out of the lake and
settled on the grass to dry off again. Soon, Donald
Duck's nephews, Huey, Dewey, and Louie, came by
in their sailboat.

"Hey, Mickey," called Dewey. "Would you
and Minnie like to borrow our boat and go sailing?
There's a good wind today."

"I've always wanted to try sailing!" said Minnie excitedly. "It's supposed to be a lot of fun."

So Mickey and Minnie hopped into the triplets' boat and took off.

"Aah, this is the life," Mickey said.

"At last, a nice, easy boat ride," said Minnie.

Just then, the wind stopped blowing.

"Oh, no!" Mickey groaned. "We're stranded again!"

Mickey and Minnie tried to paddle with their hands, but it was no use. They just kept going in circles.

Suddenly, Mickey looked up. Goofy and Donald were coming toward them in rowboats.

"We thought you might need some help," said Donald.

As the sun began to set over the peaceful lake,
Mickey and Minnie sat back and relaxed. They had
*finally* gotten their nice, easy boat ride!

# DISNEY

# MINNIE MOUSE
# THE KITTEN SITTERS

"**G**uess what?" Mickey Mouse said to his nephews, Morty and Ferdie. "We're going to watch Minnie's kitten, Figaro, while she visits her cousin. Isn't that exciting?"

Before Morty and Ferdic could answer, Minnie
and Figaro arrived. Suddenly, the boys heard wild
clucking, flapping, and crowing coming from next door
and Pluto came racing across the lawn. A big, angry
rooster followed close behind him.

"Pluto!" Minnie scolded. "Chasing chickens again! Aren't you ashamed?"

Pluto *was* a bit ashamed, but only because he had let the rooster bully him.

"It's a good thing Figaro is staying with you," Minnie told Mickey as she got into her car. "Maybe he can teach Pluto how to behave!"

Minnie was hardly out of sight when Figaro leaped out of Mickey's arms and scampered into the kitchen. With one quick hop, he jumped onto the table and knocked over a pitcher of cream.

Pluto growled at the kitten, but Mickey just cleaned up the mess.

"Take it easy, Pluto," he said. "Figaro is our guest."

At dinnertime, Pluto ate his food the way a good
dog should. But no matter how hard Mickey and the
boys tried, Figaro wouldn't touch the special food
Minnie had left for him.

At bedtime, Figaro would not use the cushion Minnie had brought for him. Instead, he got into bed with Ferdie and tickled his ears. Finally, he bounced off to the kitchen.

"Uncle Mickey," called Morty. "Did you remember to close the kitchen window?"

"Oh, no!" cried Mickey, jumping out of bed. The kitchen window was open, and Figaro was nowhere to be seen.

Mickey and the boys searched the entire house.
They looked upstairs and downstairs, under every
chair, and even in the yard. But they couldn't find
the little kitten anywhere.

"You two stay here," Mickey told his nephews.
"Pluto and I will find Figaro."

Mickey and Pluto went to Minnie's house first, but Figaro wasn't there. Next, they went to the park down the street.

"Have you seen a little black-and-white kitten?" Mickey asked a policeman.

"I certainly have!" answered the policeman. "He was teasing the ducks by the pond!"

Mickey and Pluto hurried to the pond. Figaro
wasn't there, but they *did* find some small, muddy
footprints.

Mickey and Pluto followed the trail of footprints
to Main Street, where they met a dairy truck driver.

"Have you seen a kitten?" Mickey asked.

"Have I!" cried the driver. "He knocked over my eggs!"

Mickey groaned as he paid for the broken eggs. Where was Figaro?

Mickey and Pluto searched the whole town, but there was no sign of the kitten. By the time they returned home, the sun was starting to rise.

Soon Minnie drove up. "Where is Figaro?" she asked.

No one answered.

"Something has happened to him!" Minnie cried. "Can't I trust you to watch *one* sweet little kitten?"

Just then, there was a loud clucking from the yard next door. A dozen frantic hens came flapping over the fence, with Figaro close behind.

"There's your sweet little kitten!" exclaimed Mickey. "He ran away last night and teased the ducks in the park. Then he broke the eggs in the dairy truck and—"

"And now he's chasing chickens!" Minnie finished.

"I had hoped Figaro would teach Pluto some manners," Minnie said. "Instead, Pluto has been teaching him to misbehave! I'll never leave him here again."

"Pluto didn't do anything wrong," Ferdie said.

But Minnie wouldn't listen. She picked up Figaro and quickly drove away.

"Don't worry, boys," said Mickey. "We'll tell her the whole story later, when she's not so upset."

"Please don't tell her too soon," begged Morty. "As long as Aunt Minnie thinks Pluto is a bad dog, we won't have to kitten-sit Figaro."

Mickey smiled and said, "Maybe we *should* wait a little while. We could all use some peace and quiet." And with that, he and Pluto settled down for a well-deserved nap.

# MINNIE MOUSE
# A SUMMER DAY

It was a hot summer day. Mickey Mouse and his friends were relaxing in his living room. The friends were just deciding what to do with their day when *pop*! Mickey's air-conditioning broke!

"Maybe there will be a
breeze outside," said Minnie.
But there was no breeze. Just
nice, cool lemonade from Mickey's
refrigerator.

"What are we going to do now?" asked Daisy.

Minnie looked around. "Hmmm . . ." she said.

"Maybe we could make fans. Or we could try sitting

in the shade under the tree. . . ."

"Gosh! Those sprinklers look nice and cool!"
said Goofy, pointing down at Mickey's lawn.

Donald nodded. "But there isn't enough water
coming out of them to keep *us* cool!" he said.

As Minnie watched her friends looking at the
sprinklers, she suddenly had an idea.

Minnie jumped out of her chair. "I've got it!" she shouted. "Let's go to the lake! There's always a breeze there, and there's so much to do!"

"What a great idea!" said Mickey.

"It *is* the perfect day for a swim," Daisy added.

Minnie and her friends raced home to pack. Minnie quickly threw her bathing suit and a towel into her bag. Then she headed back to Mickey's house.

In no time, the friends were on their way. They were so excited for their day at the lake!

"What should we do first?" Minnie asked.
Everyone had a different idea. Daisy wanted to
play basketball. Mickey and Pluto wanted to play
fetch. And Donald wanted to go fishing!

Before anyone could stop him,
Donald raced off toward a little boat
docked beside the water.

Donald was about to hop into the boat when
Minnie called out to him. "Wait up, Donald," she
said. "I don't think we can all fit in the boat. Let's do
something together!"

"But the water looks so nice!" said Donald.

"Why don't we go for a swim?" said Minnie. "We
can *all* do that!"

Donald wanted to go fishing, but finally he agreed. After all, they *had* come to the lake to go swimming.

The friends put away their toys and jumped into the water. . . .

"Aah," said Donald. "You were right, Minnie. This *was* a good idea!"

Minnie smiled to herself. She was glad she and her friends had found a way to cool off.

"I could stay in this water all day!" Daisy said.

And that is just what they did.

As the sun set and the day started to get cooler,
Minnie and her friends got out of the water.
Minnie had one last surprise for her friends . . . s'mores!

"Gee, Minnie," said Mickey as they roasted marshmallows over a campfire, "you really do know how to plan the perfect day!"

Finally, it really *was* time to leave.
Minnie and her friends packed their bags
and got into the car.

"That was so much fun!" said Donald
as they drove home. "Let's do it again
tomorrow!"

# DISNEY

## MICKEY MOUSE

# THE BIRTHDAY SURPRISE

Mickey woke up and jumped out of bed.
As he slipped his feet into his slippers, he said good
morning to Pluto, just like he did every day.

Mickey ate his breakfast, like he did every day. He brushed his teeth, like he did every day. And he did his stretches, like he did every day. But today was not like every other day.

Today was Mickey's birthday!

"What should we do today?" Mickey
asked Pluto.

But Pluto wasn't paying attention to
Mickey. He was staring out the window.

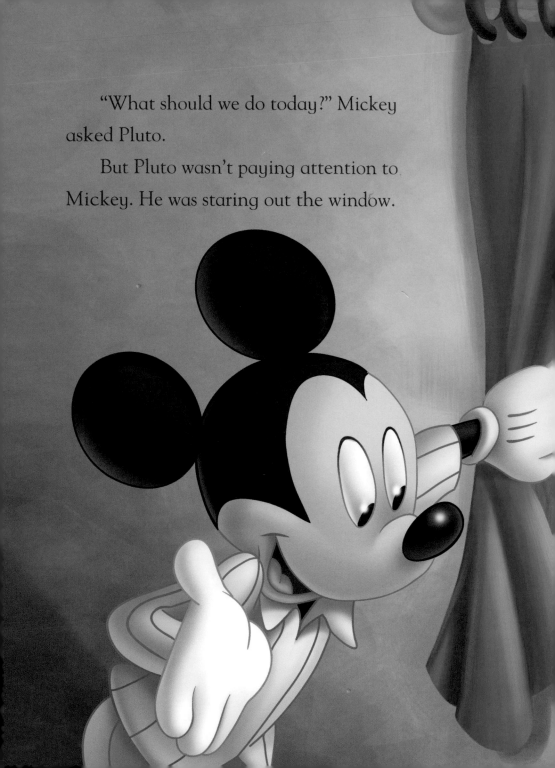

Mickey looked out the window, too.
His friends were walking past his house.
I wonder what they're doing, Mickey
thought.

Mickey looked closer. Donald was carrying cups and plates. Daisy was carrying lemonade. Goofy was carrying a bunch of balloons. And Minnie was carrying a big cake.

"Pluto!" Mickey shouted. "It looks like they're having a party!"

Mickey looked out the window again. "Do you think they know it's my birthday? Could they be having a birthday party . . . for me?"

"We'd better get dressed, Pluto," Mickey said. "Just in case!"

So Mickey dusted off his gloves and polished his buttons. He even brushed Pluto.

Soon, they were ready.

Mickey and Pluto sat in the living room and waited for their friends. And waited . . . and waited. But no one came.

Finally, the doorbell rang. Mickey jumped up
and raced to the door. He threw it open, ready for his
party. But there was no party outside. There was only
Donald. And he looked upset.

"What's wrong, Donald?" Mickey asked.

"My favorite hammock is broken," Donald told Mickey. "What am I going to do? I can't nap without it! Can you help me fix it?"

Mickey knew his friend needed his help. "Sure, Donald," he said. "Let's go!"

So Donald, Mickey, and Pluto set off to fix the hammock. As they walked, an idea popped into Mickey's head.

Maybe there *is* no broken hammock, he thought. Maybe Donald is *really* taking me to my party!

Mickey was so excited that he started to skip.

Donald led Mickey into his front yard. He
stopped in front of two trees and looked down. There,
on the ground, was the broken hammock.

Mickey looked around. There were no balloons and no cake. There was just one friend who needed his help. So Mickey helped Donald fix his hammock.

"That should do it," Mickey said as he finished tying the hammock's rope around a tree.

"Thanks, Mickey!" Donald said when the hammock was strung up between the trees again. Donald climbed into his hammock and was soon drifting off to sleep.

"You're welcome," Mickey said, and he started to head home.

I guess there wasn't a party after all, Mickey
thought. Just then, he heard Minnie and Daisy calling
him. They wanted to show him something!

So Mickey went with Minnie and Daisy. As he
walked, Mickey began to wonder about a party again.

Maybe *they* are taking me to my party! he
thought.

Minnie and Daisy led Mickey to their flower garden.

"Ta-da!" said Daisy.

"Everything is blooming!" said Minnie.

Mickey looked around. The garden was full of flowers. And they *were* pretty. Still, Mickey couldn't help but be disappointed.

"Do you want to help us garden?" Minnie asked.

Mickey thought about it. He didn't have any other plans. So he helped water the flowers.

A few minutes later, Goofy ran up.

"Mickey! Mickey!" he shouted, tugging on his friend's arm. "You've got to see this. I've never seen anything like it!"

Mickey waved good-bye to Minnie and Daisy and rushed away with Goofy.

Goofy seems very excited, Mickey thought as his friend rushed him down the road. I wonder what he wants to show me.

Then Mickey realized, Goofy must be taking him to his party!

Suddenly, Goofy stopped running.

"Look, Mickey," he said, pointing to a large rock.

Mickey looked all around, but there was no sign of a party. Why was Goofy so excited?

Then Mickey looked down. Two snails were racing on the rock.

"Gosh! Watch 'em go!" Goofy said. "Have you ever seen anything so exciting?"

Mickey had never seen a snail race before. It was exciting, but not as exciting as a party!

Mickey and Pluto watched the snails race for a while. Then they headed home.

"Oh, well, Pluto," Mickey said. "I guess I was wrong. I guess there won't be a party after all.

Pluto whimpered. He had never seen Mickey look so sad.

Mickey hung his head low. How could everyone have forgotten his birthday?

Mickey walked up the path to his house. He opened the front door and stepped inside.

As he reached for the light switch . . .

"Surprise!"

Mickey's friends jumped out at him. They had
planned a party after all. A surprise party! For the
first time all day, Mickey had not expected it.

"I don't understand," he said. "I thought you were all busy today. How did you find time to plan a party . . . at my house . . . without me finding out?"

Minnie giggled. "We took turns keeping you busy," she explained.

"Hyuck," Goofy laughed. "You didn't even realize we were planning a party. I guess we're pretty sneaky!"

Mickey thought about his day. . . .
Donald's broken hammock . . .
Daisy and Minnie's flowers . . .
Goofy's snail race . . .
Now Mickey understood.

Mickey smiled a huge smile. He was glad his
friends had tricked him. He loved surprise parties!

"Thanks, everyone," Mickey said, "for the best
party ever! And the best birthday!"

Mickey's friends clapped and cheered, "Happy
birthday, Mickey!"